On the Day I Was Born

by Debbi Chocolate

Illustrated by Melodye Rosales

SCHOLASTIC INC. Cartwheel B·O·O·K·S ®

New York Toronto London Auckland Sydney

Chocolate, Deborah M. Newton.
    On the day I was born / Debbi Chocolate ; illustrated by Melodye Rosales.
        p.   cm.
    Summary: Members of an extended African American family celebrate with joy and pride the birth of a firstborn son.
    ISBN 0-590-47609-2
    [1. Babies—Fiction.   2. Afro-Americans—Fiction.   3. Family life—Fiction.]   I. Rosales, Melodye, ill.   II. Title.
    PZ7.C44624On   1995
    [Fic]—dc20   94-40994
                                                                                                                CIP
                                                                                                                AC

12 11 10 9 8 7 6 5 4 3 2 1   5 6 7 8 9/9 0/0

Printed in the U.S.A.   37

First Scholastic printing, October 1995

For my boys, Bobby Jr. and Allen Whitney Chocolate,
who were both held up to the full moon's light.
—D.C.

Special thanks to Chuck Mercer Photography—Urbana, IL; Professor William Berry for
introducing me to Chuck; Bruce Nesbitt—Director Afro-American Cultural Center, U.I.
Champaign, IL, for all your help; Chris Benson for all your devotion, and Kaye Benson for
always listening; to my mom, who is always there for me; and to my loving family—Giraldo,
Giraldo Jr., Harmony, and Symphony—this is for you.
—M.R.

African Adinkra symbols, created by the Asante people of Ghana to decorate cloth, have been used as a design element in this book. The symbols and their meanings are:

 Security in the home

 Defiance (the fern)

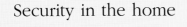 Human relations—
"We are linked together."

 Changing one's self;
playing many parts

 Good fortune

"You can always undo
your mistakes."

Slavery (handcuffs)

Strength (the ram's horns)

 Unity—"Bite not one
another."

 Forgiveness

 Humility—"Be not boastful
or arrogant."

The presence of God
(an altar to the sky god)

Melodye Rosales

Melodye Rosales's Source for Adinkra Symbols
source: Dawn Blackman, Motherland Art and Design

In January 1977, I watched Kunta Kinte hold his firstborn daughter up to the light of the moon in the epic film *Roots*, based on Alex Haley's acclaimed book of the same title. I did not realize how deeply that image had touched me until the birth of my own first child.

On the day my son was born, I asked my husband to hold him up to the light of the moon, just as Kunta Kinte had done. A few days after his birth, our son was presented with a kente cloth, which we set aside for him until his twelfth birthday. One year later, our second son was born. To maintain our newfound traditions, he, too, was held up to the moonlight and received a kente cloth of his own.

Cherished memories of my own roots and the arrival of my two sons led to my writing this book. I hope that as you read it, you discover, as I have, that family traditions are something children can take part in with eagerness—and pride.

Peace and love,

Debbi Chocolate

On the day I was born,
Daddy held me up to
the full moon's light.

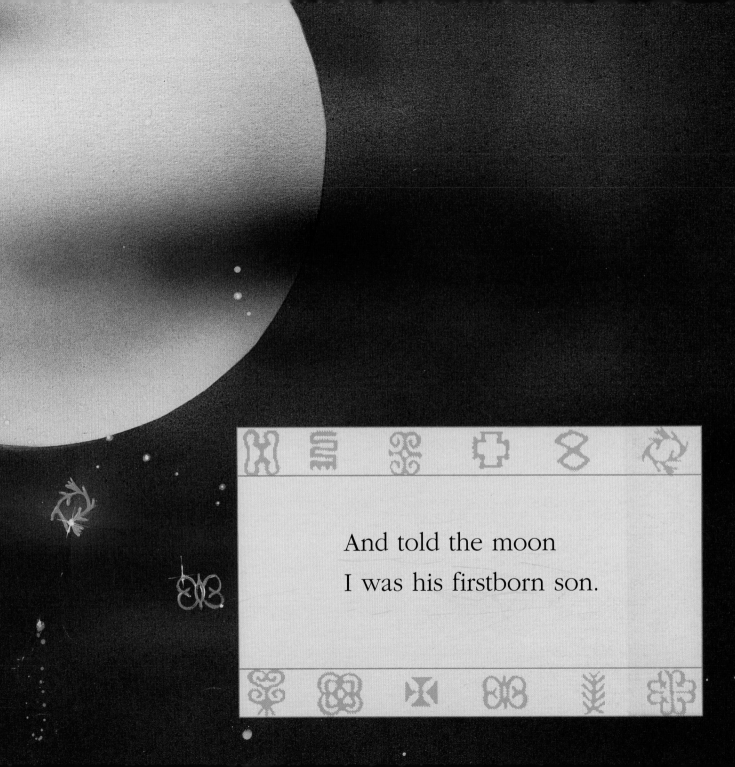

And told the moon
I was his firstborn son.

On the day I was born,

Mama wrapped me in a soft cloth.

I got a kofia, or crown.

And lots and lots of soft, warm hugs.

On the day I was born,
Uncle Preedy blessed me.
Aunt Alma named me.

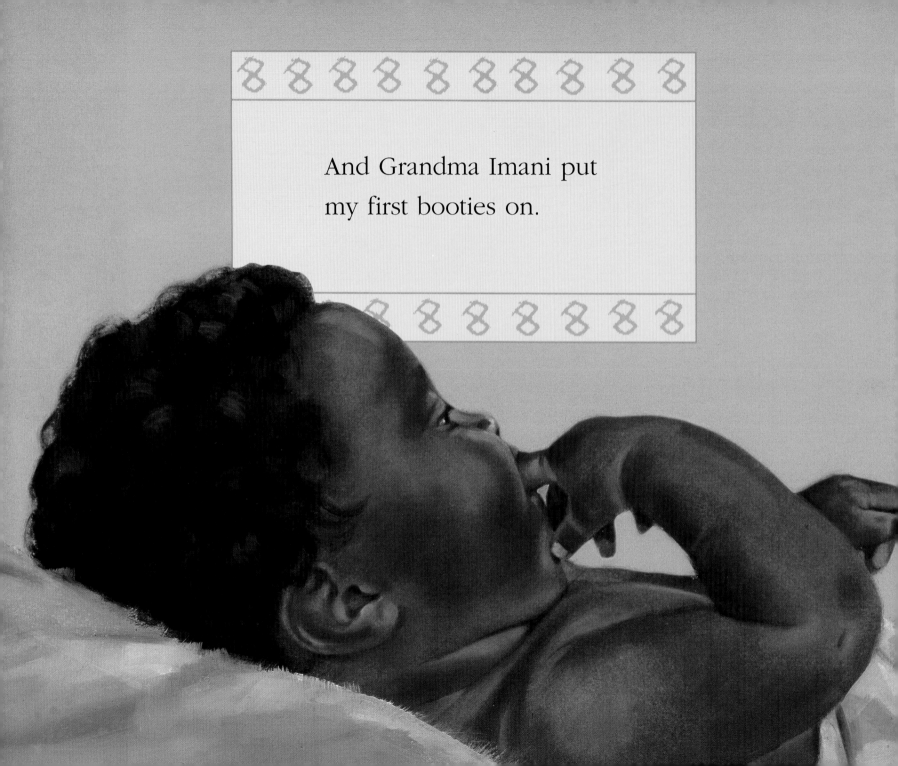

And Grandma Imani put
my first booties on.

On the day I was born,
there was lots of talk
of who I looked like.

Did I look more like Cousin Tom?
Uncle Albert?

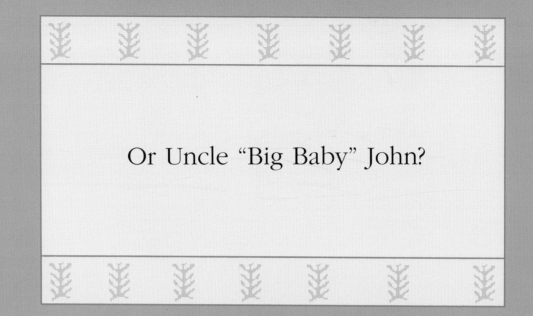

Or Uncle "Big Baby" John?

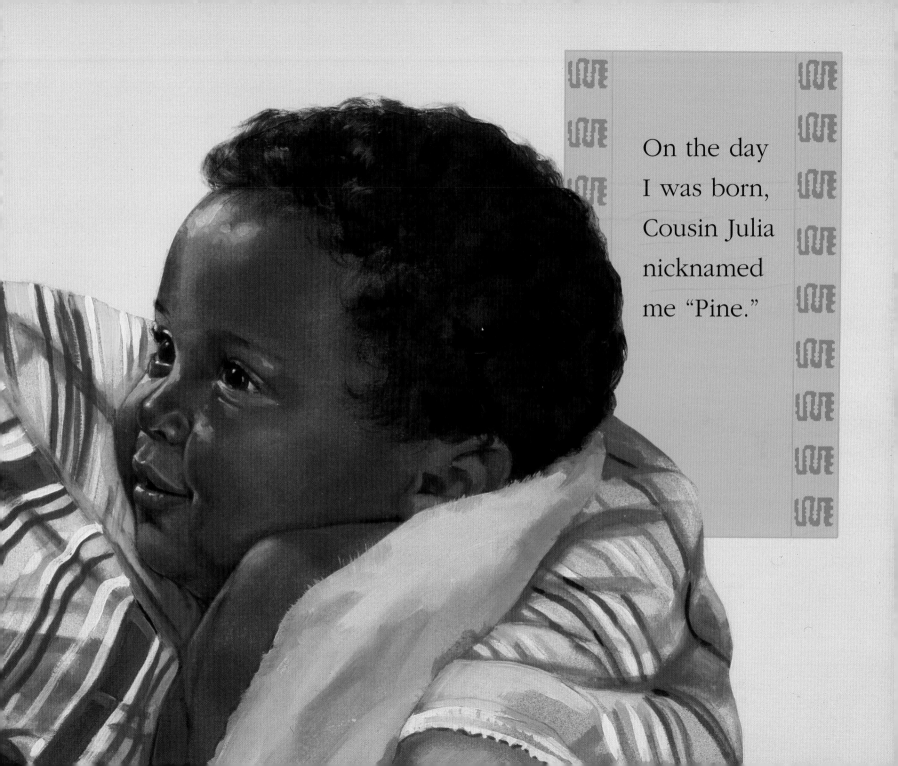

On the day
I was born,
Cousin Julia
nicknamed
me "Pine."

On the day I was born,
a kente cloth was given to me
to wear when I am old enough.

On the day I was born,
my father stood tall.
And so did his father.

On the day I was born,
my daddy held me up to the heavens.

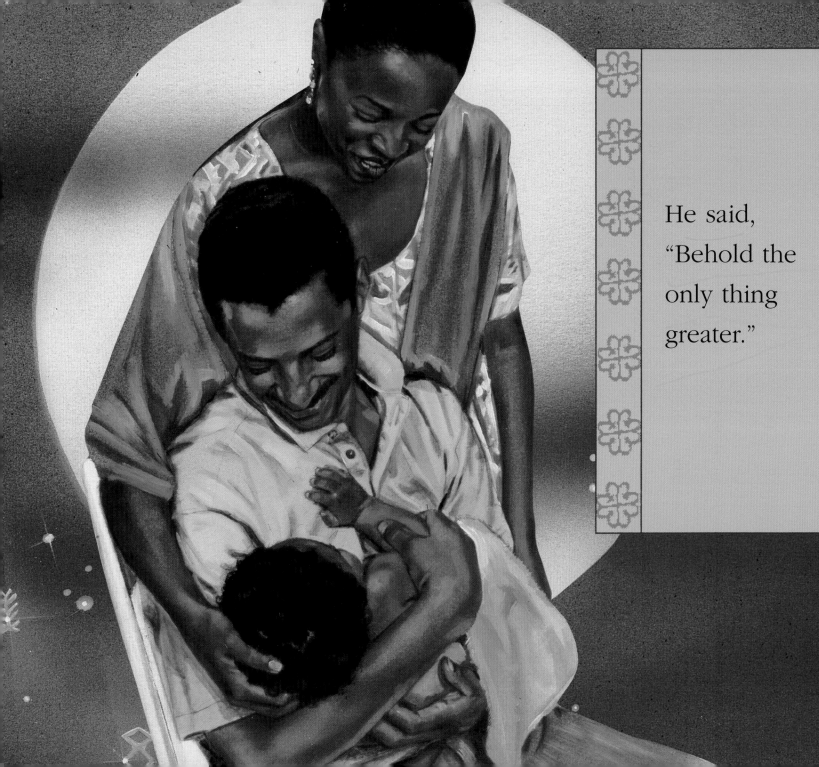

He said,
"Behold the
only thing
greater."

DATE DUE